Fall
Leaves
Fall!

by ZOE HALL

illustrated by

SHARI HALPERN

Scholastic Press · New York

For Lauren

Text copyright © 2000 by Zoe Hall
Illustrations copyright © 2000 by Shari Halpern
All rights reserved. Published by Scholastic Press, a division of Scholastic Inc., *Publishers since 1920*.
SCHOLASTIC and SCHOLASTIC PRESS and associated logos are trademarks and/or registered trademarks of
Scholastic Inc. No part of this publication may be reproduced, or stored in a retrieval system, or transmitted
in any form or by any means, electronic, mechanical, photocopying, recording, or otherwise, without written
permission of the publisher. For information regarding permission, write to Scholastic Inc., Attention:
Permissions Department, 555 Broadway, New York, NY 10012.

Library of Congress Cataloging-in-Publication Data available. Library of Congress number: 98-26536
ISBN 0-590-10079-3
10 9 8 7 6 5 4   02 03 04
Printed in Mexico   49
First edition, October 2000

JJ
HALL
ZOE

The text type was set in 25.5 point Worcester Medium.
The artist used painted and found papers to create collage illustrations for this book.
Book design by Kristina Albertson

All year long, my brother and I
wait for our favorite season to come.
Can you guess what it is?

Fall!

How do we know when fall is coming?

We watch the leaves.
In summer, the leaves on the trees are green.

When the leaves change color,
we know fall is here.

Look at all the fall colors!
Leaves turn red, orange, and yellow.

When the wind blows,
leaves start to fall from the trees.

We try to catch them.

We like to stomp on the leaves — *CRUNCH!*
We like to kick the leaves, too.
All the fall colors fly back into the air.

We like to collect leaves.
Some leaves are very small.
Some leaves are big!

Some leaves have pointy edges.

Some leaves have smooth edges.

When the leaves cover the ground,
it's time to rake them up.

At last, we have made a HUGE pile.
Next, . . .

. . . we jump in!

Inside, we drink mugs of warm cider and eat lots of cookies.

maple

sassafras

oak

These leaves came from our favorite trees.

ginkgo

beech

oak
too!

We make pictures with our leaves.

Before long,
the leaves have turned brown
and the branches are bare.

All the fall colors are gone.
But we know they will be
back next year!

How leaves grow through the year:

1. In spring, small buds on tree branches open and tiny, light-green leaves appear. They grow bigger every day.

2. By summer, the leaves have grown to full size and are deep green. The leaves use sunlight to make food for the tree.

3. In fall, the green color fades and bright fall colors appear. The leaf stems weaken, and the leaves fall off the branches.

4. In winter, all of the leaves have fallen off. The tree makes buds, which will become new leaves in the spring.

Some leaves, such as needles on pine trees, do not change color and do not fall off in fall. Which fall colors do you see where you live?